The Polar Bear Express

★ Also by ★
Debbie Dadey

Mermaid Tales

Book 1: *Trouble at Trident Academy*

Book 2: *Battle of the Best Friends*

Book 3: *A Whale of a Tale*

Book 4: *Danger in the Deep Blue Sea*

Book 5: *The Lost Princess*

Book 6: *The Secret Sea Horse*

Book 7: *Dream of the Blue Turtle*

Book 8: *Treasure in Trident City*

Book 9: *A Royal Tea*

Book 10: *A Tale of Two Sisters*

Coming Soon

Book 12: *Wish upon a Starfish*

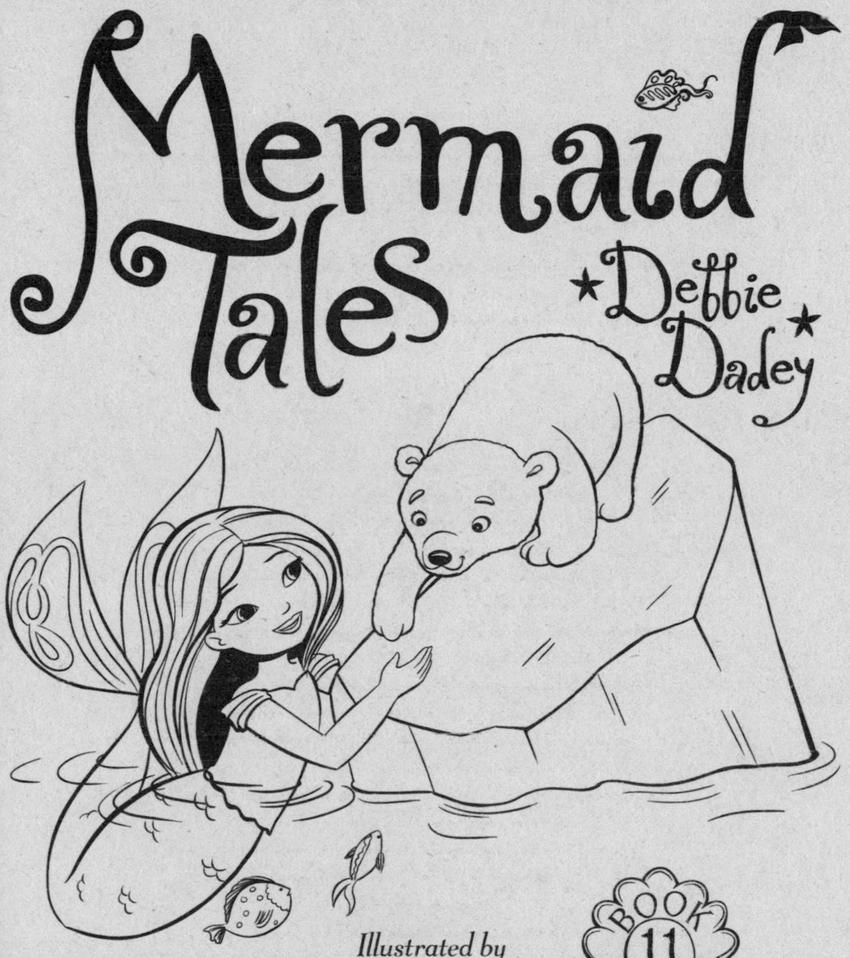

Illustrated by
Tatevik Avakyan

The Polar Bear Express

ALADDIN
NEW YORK LONDON TORONTO SYDNEY NEW DELHI

ALADDIN
An imprint of Simon & Schuster Children's Publishing Division
1230 Avenue of the Americas, New York, NY 10020
This Aladdin paperback edition May 2015

Also available in an Aladdin hardcover edition.

Book design by Karin Paprocki
The text of this book was set in Belucian Book.
Manufactured in the United States of America 0117 OFF
4 6 8 10 9 7 5 3
Library of Congress Control Number 2014937344
ISBN 978-1-4814-0261-3 (hc)
ISBN 978-1-4814-0260-6 (pbk)
ISBN 978-1-4814-0262-0 (eBook)

To Nancy Crowther, Sybil Johnson,
Pete Brunner, Marijane Meckling,
Sue Goldsworthy, Bob Scofield,
and all my Moland House friends

★ ★ ★ ★

Acknowledgment

Thanks to summer intern Hannah Frank for haiku brainstorming.

N
E
S
W
The Mayor's House
Pearl's Home
Trident School for Languages
Trident City Hall
Big Rock Cafe
Trident Academy
Trident Plaza Hotel
The Coral Reef
56
Reef 56 Hotel
Merlin's
Angel Fish Antiques

Kelp Fields
Echo's House
Peeple Museum • Shelly's Home
Manta Ray Station
Reef's Fish Store
er Park
Little V
Whale Mountain
Big V
Trident City

Cast of Characters
Shelly
Echo
Kiki
Pearl
Rocky

Contents

The Polar Bear Express

1

Splat!

"Five arms stretch out wide

No brains; no blood; velvety

Starfish cling to life."

"I really like that," Kiki Coral told her teacher.

"It's a haiku," Mrs. Karp explained.

"Five claps for the first line, then seven, then five for the last line."

"Boring," Pearl Swamp whispered under her breath. Mrs. Karp peered through her tiny glasses at Pearl, who slid down in her seat.

"Do you think the Rays' music is boring?" Mrs. Karp asked Pearl.

Pearl sat up straight and tossed her long blond hair behind her shoulder. "Of course not!" The Rays were the most famous boy band in the ocean. They had sung at Pearl's last birthday party.

"Did you know that many of the Rays' songs are poems?" Mrs. Karp said. "Of course, they are different from a haiku."

"Really?" asked Shelly Siren. Shelly was the only student at Trident Academy who had actually performed with the Rays at Pearl's party. When their backup singer had gotten sick, Shelly had filled in for her.

Mrs. Karp nodded and surprised her entire third-grade class by singing one of the Rays' songs.

"Shark, the sharpnose sevengill,
lived near to me.
We swam together every day
And became the best of friends.

Then someone told Shark he
should eat me.
And now I miss him terribly
But our friendship had to end.
Shark, the sharpnose sevengill,
lived near to me.
I'll always treasure our friendship
And hope someday he'll see
That sharks and merfolks can be friends.
One day it will be.
But until that day, I guess I'll say
Shark, I miss you still."

Pearl rolled her eyes, but most of the class tapped their tails in time to Mrs. Karp's voice. When she finished, everyone clapped except Pearl.

"That was totally amazing!" Echo Reef said.

Mrs. Karp grinned and took a little bow. "What do you think about poems now?" she asked Pearl.

Pearl shrugged. "I guess some poems are pretty wavy."

"I think poems should be silly," Rocky Ridge said before singing to the class in a funny voice:

"Food fights can be fun.
Especially at lunchtime.
Splat! Right in the face!"

Rocky acted out the splat and fell onto the floor.

Mrs. Karp hid her smile behind her hand, but Kiki couldn't help laughing just a little. "That was very creative," Mrs. Karp told Rocky, "but I hope you don't plan to have a real food fight."

Rocky shook his head, but Kiki noticed the grin on his face. Kiki knew Rocky would love to throw anything, especially food.

"You've given me a wonderful idea," Mrs. Karp told Rocky. "Everyone will write their own poem for our next class assignment. It can be a haiku or a song or whatever type you'd like. We'll talk about other kinds of poems in class tomorrow."

Pearl frowned at Rocky. "Thanks a lot!" she snapped. "More homework!"

2

Shake Your Tail

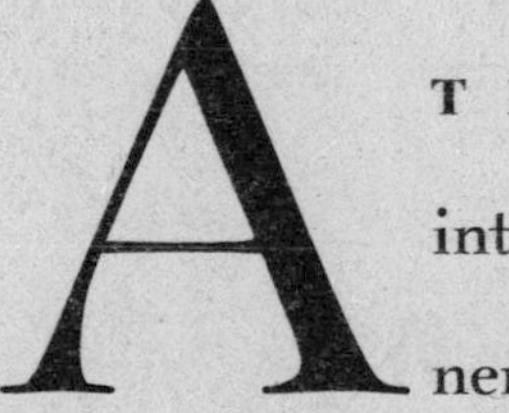

AT LUNCHTIME KIKI SLID into a round table in a corner of Trident Academy's cafeteria. Shelly and their merfriend Echo joined her.

"Wasn't it fun when Mrs. Karp sang in class?" Kiki asked.

Shelly smiled. "I didn't know she had such a nice voice."

"I love that Rays song," Echo said. "Have you heard their newest one?"

Kiki shook her head, pushed her long black hair out of her face, and took a bite of her crab casserole.

"Sing it for her, Shelly," Echo said, giving Shelly a little nudge with her shoulder.

Shelly sang,

"Shake your tail
Shake, shake, shake your tail
Let's bubble down and make like a
whale
Shake, shake, shake your tail."

Shelly was probably the best singer in the whole school—maybe in the entire merkingdom. She was so good that everyone in the cafeteria stopped to listen to her. When Shelly finished, Kiki clapped and the rest of the school joined in. Everyone but Pearl.

Shelly's face turned red. She quickly scooped up a big bite of her longhorn cowfish and ate it without looking up. Her long hair partly covered her crimson cheeks.

Pearl floated over to their table and pointed her nose up in the water. "Did you know that the Rays are performing a concert in Poseidon tomorrow?"

"Really?" Echo asked. Poseidon was the town right next to Trident City, where they lived.

KELP
CHIPS

Pearl nodded. "Yes, and my father is taking me to see them. I bet I'm the only one in the whole school who will go. The tickets are very expensive."

Shelly, Echo, and Kiki looked at one another without saying a word. Pearl's parents were rich, and they lived in one of Trident City's biggest shells. Everyone knew Pearl always got want she wanted. Many Trident City merfolk thought Pearl's parents spoiled her.

Kiki felt like telling Pearl that it wasn't nice to brag, but Pearl wasn't finished. "I'm going to write the Rays a poem song. I'll give it to them, and I bet they'll sing it just for me."

"That's great idea," Echo said.

Kiki looked at Echo in surprise. Kiki

knew Echo didn't like Pearl's bragging either.

"I'm going to write a poem song too," Echo continued. "Maybe the Rays will like mine and make it famous throughout the merworld."

Pearl frowned. "But I thought of it first!"

Pearl's friend Wanda swam up beside Pearl. "It *is* a great idea. I'm going to write a song for the Rays too."

Pearl gave Wanda a dirty look and swam off to her own table, leaving a trail of bubbles behind. Wanda followed with a worried look on her face.

"Let's meet at my shell after school," Shelly told her friends. "We can work on our poems and poem songs together."

"I can bring the snacks," Kiki suggested. "I just got a trunk full of treats from home. My mom sent lots of sea cucumbers."

Unlike Shelly and Echo, who lived close to Trident Academy, Kiki's family lived far across the ocean, so she stayed in the school's dormitory. Kiki's mom often sent her care packages filled with goodies.

Shelly grinned. "Yum! I love those!"

"Oops!" Kiki said. "I forgot that I have vision practice with Madame Hippocampus after school today."

"Just come over when you're done," Shelly said.

"Hey, do you know the best part about writing a poem song for the Rays?" Echo asked her friends.

"What?" Kiki asked.

"Making Pearl mad without even trying," Echo replied with a giggle.

All three girls turned to look at Pearl. She was staring at them from across the room with a big frown on her face.

"Oh my Neptune!" Shelly said. "We don't want to make Pearl angry at us."

Kiki nodded. "Pearl does seem to like trouble."

Echo shrugged. "I know, but how much trouble could she *really* cause us?"

3 Visions

I WISH I DIDN'T HAVE TO STAY AFTER school," Kiki told Shelly and Echo as the conch shell sounded to end the day. They floated into the huge front hallway of Trident Academy. Students in grades three through ten zipped past them on their way to after-school activities, their dorm rooms, or home.

"Well, *I* wish I could see the future like you," Echo said. Only a few mermaids actually had the gift of foresight.

"You *are* lucky to be able to have visions," Shelly agreed. "And we'll see you at my shell after your lesson."

Kiki sighed. She wasn't sure that being able to view the future was a good thing. After all, she only had visions every once in a while. Plus, sometimes they were scary, like the time she thought she saw Rocky getting hurt by a huge turtle. Luckily, it turned out that the turtle was actually saving Rocky, not hurting him!

"See you soon," Kiki said as she floated away from the main hall, past the library, and toward Madame Hippocampus's classroom.

Madame Hippocampus chuckled when Kiki swam into the room. "I knew you were coming!" Madame said.

Kiki smiled. It was their usual joke, since Madame could see the future too. During the school day, Madame taught merology, the study of merfolk life, including history, government, and society. After school, she gave vision lessons. Some merstudents were shocked by Madame's looks—she had a horse's head and dolphin's tail—but Kiki had been taking vision lessons for several months. Now she was used to being taught by a hippocampus.

"Today we will work on making your

visions come whenever you want," Madame said. "First you need to close your eyes and concentrate. Clear your thoughts. Open your mind."

Kiki shut her eyes. She tried to clear her head, but thoughts kept coming. She imagined going over to Shelly's shell. She wondered what kind of poem she should write for class.

Madame neighed. "Kiki, stop thinking and make your mind blank."

"I'm trying," Kiki said. She knew Madame could sometimes read her mind. Kiki did try not to think, but she didn't have much success at making a vision appear. She only managed to see that the Trident Academy cafeteria would serve ribbon worms for lunch tomorrow. Anyone could have guessed that!

After a half hour, Madame tapped a hoof on her marble desk and said, "That's all the time we have for now. Let's try again next week."

Kiki popped open her eyes. "Thanks!" she called as she darted out of the room. She couldn't wait to get to Shelly's apartment.

Kiki loved any chance to get away from school. Living in the dorm was fun, but it could get lonely being so far away from her family. She dashed to her room, grabbed the small trunk of treats her mom had sent, and scooted out the front door.

Kiki swam through MerPark without a thought in her head. Just as she passed the Manta Ray Express Station, where enormous manta rays took merpeople anywhere in the whole wide ocean, Kiki's eyes grew cloudy and her ears clogged up. She was so startled she stopped short. She was having a vision!

In her mind she saw something unusual in the water above her. When the vision was over, Kiki couldn't resist looking up. When she did, she got the surprise of her life!

4 Nestor

A STRANGE SHAPE SPLASHED in the water overhead. Kiki squinted her eyes to make out a furry white foot with black toenails. She was so startled she started to scream, but one word stopped her. "*Help!*"

Kiki knew she had heard that language

before. She thought very hard and said, *"Can I help you?"*

Immediately the foot stopped moving. In seconds a white face with a black nose appeared in front of Kiki. She couldn't believe her eyes. It was a baby polar bear!

"You can speak my language?" the little bear asked.

Kiki nodded. She tried to remember whether polar bears ate mermaids. She was pretty sure they didn't but decided not to get too close just in case.

"Are you a mermaid? You won't hurt me, will you?" The little bear sniffed the water.

Kiki smiled. "*I'm Kiki and I am a mermaid, but I won't hurt you.*"

"*My name is Nestor, and I'm lost,*" said the little bear. "*Can you help me find my home?*"

"*But I've never heard of a polar bear in Trident City before,*" Kiki said slowly, still keeping her distance.

"*I fell asleep on a piece of ice. When I woke up, I had floated far away from home. Now my ice has almost melted, and I have nowhere to go. I'm really hungry and scared.*" Nestor's eyes filled with tears, and Kiki knew he wasn't dangerous.

Without hesitation she opened her trunk of goodies. "*Here, take these.*" Out floated the sea cucumbers that Shelly liked so much, some crab popovers, octopus legs, and delicious-looking sea-slug sushi. Kiki hoped her merfriends wouldn't be mad that she'd given away the treats, but she felt sorry for the hungry little bear.

Nestor took one sniff and opened his mouth wide. Kiki floated backward as he gobbled the goodies down in a mersecond. Nestor then swam up to the surface and Kiki thought he was gone for good.

"*Thanks,*" Nestor said, swimming back beside her. "*I feel better now. Do you know the way home?*"

Kiki shook her head. "*I'm sorry. I don't.*"

Nestor's lip trembled, and tears rolled down his furry white cheeks. "*But I want to see my mommy.*"

Even though Nestor was almost as big as

a mermaid, Kiki could tell he was still very young. She wanted to help him, but how?

"I don't know how to get you home, but I'll find out. Can you wait for me while I get help?"

Nestor nodded. Kiki darted to Shelly's apartment as quickly as she could.

"Fin-tastic," Echo said as Kiki swam through the door. "You're here! Where are the snacks?"

"I don't have them anymore," Kiki explained. "I gave them away."

"You gave away the sea cucumbers?" Shelly asked. "But I'm starving!"

"I gave them to a polar bear," Kiki said.

Echo laughed. "No, really, where are they?"

"I'm serious," Kiki said. "On the way

over here I saw a baby polar bear in the water. He was lost and hungry, so I gave him my snacks."

"A real polar bear?" Shelly asked. "I've never seen one."

Echo's eyes grew wide. "Are you teasing us?"

Kiki shook her head.

"Aren't polar bears dangerous?" Echo gasped.

Shelly nodded. "You shouldn't get close to one. It could eat you for a snack."

"This one was really little," Kiki told them.

"But polar bears and mermaids don't live anywhere near each other," Echo said. "It must be some other creature."

Kiki shook her head. "No, it was definitely a polar bear." She turned to Shelly. "Is your grandfather here?"

"No, he's downstairs in the museum," Shelly said. "He has a very important meeting with a humanologist and told me not to interrupt."

"Oh my Neptune!" Kiki exclaimed. "What are we going to do now?"

Shelly's grandfather ran the Trident City People Museum, and he was quite wise. Kiki had hoped he would know how to get Nestor home.

"What's wrong?" Echo asked.

"The bear is in trouble! His patch of ice is melting, and soon he'll have nowhere to go. I think he needs our help," Kiki explained. "He's not dangerous. He's just a baby. I promise."

"Then we'd better go see him right now," Shelly said. "Show us the way!"

"Come on," Kiki said, forgetting all about the poems they were supposed to write. Helping the little bear was much more important. The girls dashed back to the place where Nestor had been, but he was gone!

"Where is he?" Kiki cried. She hoped that nothing terrible had happened to the little bear.

5

Down to Business

KIKI LOOKED ALL AROUND the Manta Ray Station, where she had seen Nestor. Several manta rays were lined up, waiting to take merfolk to their destinations. But the little polar bear was nowhere to be found. "Where could he be?" she asked her merfriends.

"If Nestor is a polar bear, then I don't think he can breathe underwater," Shelly said slowly. "He probably had to go back to the surface for air." All three girls looked up toward the top of the water, but they couldn't see anything that looked like a polar bear.

Echo nodded. "I think Shelly is right, but we can find out for sure at the library. I bet they have lots of books about polar bears."

Shelly grabbed Kiki's hand. "Come on, the Trident City Library is this way."

The three mergirls swam through MerPark to the back of Trident City Hall. They passed between the marble pillars that lined the entrance to the oldest library in the merworld.

Shelly and Echo were used to the splendor of their local library, but Kiki had never seen it before. She couldn't help staring at the pink marble walls and the sparkling diamonds that lined the ceiling in different sea-creature shapes. But most impressive of all was the vast number of rock and seaweed books that filled the shelves at the back of the library.

"I thought the front hall of Trident Academy was beautiful," Kiki gasped. "But this is shell-tacular!"

"Shhh!" said an older librarian from behind a massive granite counter. She frowned at the mergirls.

"Hey, that's Lillian!" Echo whispered.

"Who is Lillian?" Kiki asked quietly.

"Mr. Fangtooth's sweetheart," Shelly murmured. Mr. Fangtooth was their school's grumpy cafeteria worker. Recently Echo and Shelly had found a love letter that Mr. Fangtooth had written to Lillian long ago.

The girls giggled at the thought of crabby Mr. Fangtooth being in love, but then Kiki got down to business. "Where are the books about polar bears?" she asked.

Shelly knew just where to go. She led Kiki and Echo to the library's animal section. Each mergirl chose several titles about polar bears and began reading.

"You were right about polar bears," Kiki told Shelly. "They can't breathe underwater, but they can hold their breath for about two minutes."

POLAR
BEARS

"Did you know that they are in danger because of something called global warming?" Shelly told the other mergirls.

"What's that?" Echo asked.

Shelly shrugged and read further. "It has to do with exhaust pollution by humans, but I'm not sure what that is."

"Maybe it's what people breathe out," Kiki suggested.

"It says here that polar bears live in the Arctic Ocean," Echo said, pointing to a map in her book.

"Where's that?" Kiki asked, looking over Echo's shoulder.

Echo gulped. "It's a long way from here."

"The poor baby," Kiki said with tears in her eyes. "That little bear is far from home, and his mother doesn't know where he is."

"We have to help him," Shelly said.

"But what can we do?" Echo asked. "We're only in third grade."

Kiki didn't know, but she was sure of two things. First, they were going to find Nestor. Then, somehow, some way, they were going to get him home!

6
Puffer Fish

AN HOUR LATER THE THREE mergirls were still looking at books at the Trident City Library, but they weren't any closer to figuring out how to get Nestor home.

"What if we got a whole bunch of puffer fish and tied them to Nestor's feet?" Echo suggested. "That way if a gust of wind came, maybe the puffer fish could blow the little bear home." Puffer fish could take in big gulps of water and puff up to several times their regular size.

"I think you have the right idea," Shelly agreed. "Maybe we could even tie a big bird to Nestor, and the bird could pull him home."

"But what if the puffer fish or the bird took Nestor the wrong way?" Kiki asked. "Then he'd be even more lost."

"*Shhhh.*" Lillian the librarian swam up beside them and put her finger to her lips. "I don't want to have to tell you again to be quiet."

"Sorry, ma'am," Shelly said. "We were just leaving."

Lillian raised her hand. "Not so fast."

Kiki held her breath. Were they in trouble? How would they be able to help Nestor if they couldn't leave the library?

"Aren't you the mergirls who gave Mendel Fangtooth the old letter he wrote to me years ago?" Lillian asked.

Echo slowly nodded her head.

Lillian surprised Kiki by breaking into a big smile. "Then I need to thank you," the librarian said. "That letter reunited me with my true love! Because of you, Mendel and I are to be married."

"Married!" Shelly exclaimed.

"How exciting," Echo said.

"Congratulations," Kiki told Lillian.

"Since you merladies played such a big

part in helping us find each other again, you will definitely be invited to the wedding," Lillian told them. "But right now, let me know if you need help finding anything in the library. We'll be closing for the day soon."

"We're trying to figure out how to get a lost baby polar bear home," Kiki explained. "There's one near the Manta Ray Express Station."

"A polar bear in Trident City!" Lillian exclaimed. "Isn't that dangerous?"

Kiki explained that Nestor was just a baby and would never harm a merperson. "Well, I never! I have to see this!" Lillian said. "Can you show me?"

"We'll show you where I last saw him," Kiki answered.

After Lillian locked up the library, she followed the mergirls out the door toward the Manta Ray station.

"There he is!" Kiki pointed to a big white form diving above them.

"What's on his back?" Echo asked.

"It's Rocky!" Shelly yelled.

Kiki couldn't believe that Rocky was riding the bear. "Oh my Neptune!" she cried. "Rocky, get off Nestor before you hurt him!"

Rocky floated off Nestor and swam over to the mergirls. "I wasn't hurting him. He seemed nice, so I thought we'd have a little fun."

Kiki frowned at Rocky, then turned to Nestor. "*These are my friends Shelly, Echo,*

Rocky, and Miss Lillian. We're trying to find a way to get you home."

"Thanks for your help, Kiki," Nestor said with a smile. *"But I have to get back to the surface now. I need some air."*

Shelly grabbed Kiki's arm. "You know how to speak polar bear?" she asked. "Will you teach me?"

"Of course," Kiki told her friend. Kiki knew Shelly loved learning ocean languages almost as much as she did.

Lillian watched Nestor swim upward before shaking her head. "A baby polar bear in Trident City! I never would have believed

it if I hadn't seen it with my own eyes. I can't wait to tell Mendel." Lillian waved to the merkids and swam off to catch a manta ray home. Kiki watched Lillian drift away.

Echo giggled. "This is a crazy day. Mr. Fangtooth is getting married *and* we met a polar bear. Can anything weirder happen?"

"Old Mr. Fangtooth is getting married?" Rocky asked.

"Yes," Shelly said. "But the important thing now is to figure out how to save that baby polar bear. He's lost and a long way from home."

Kiki nodded. "And Lillian just gave me an idea of how to help."

"How?" Echo asked.

Kiki smiled. "Come with me and find out."

7

A Shell Wash

"HAVE SOME PARROT-FISH pancakes," Echo told Nestor the next morning.

"And some sea-squirt sausage," Shelly said. Nestor gobbled the food down in one bite.

Kiki wished she had more to offer

Nestor than her tiny bowl of clingfish cereal. Nestor swallowed that quickly too, and he even licked the shell. Kiki was worried. How long would it be before Nestor's block of ice melted and left him stranded? What if a big wave came along and took him even farther away? Living so far from home, Kiki missed her mother very much; she couldn't stand the thought of the little bear never finding his mother again.

"*See you after school,*" Kiki told Nestor.

"And we'll bring you a snack," Shelly promised. Kiki translated her words.

Nestor grinned as he swam back to the surface. The mergirls darted off to school, and Kiki told her friends how worried she was about Nestor.

"But Kiki," Shelly said, "you've already figured out how to get him home."

Echo nodded. "It's a great idea to have the Manta Ray Express take Nestor to the Arctic. The conductor said he knew exactly how to get there."

"But it doesn't matter," Kiki said, "because we don't have enough jewels to pay for his ride." She'd been excited when she'd thought of the idea that Nestor could ride home on a huge manta ray. But she had been very upset when she'd found out how much it would cost.

"Don't worry," Shelly told her. "We'll figure out how to pay for it somehow."

Later in class, Kiki was supposed to be writing her poem, but she could only think about Nestor. She tapped her purple tail on the sandy floor of the classroom and wrote:

My polar buddy
So lost in the great ocean
He needs a way home.

Kiki smiled as she read her haiku to herself. Without thinking she put her feathery sea pen in her mouth and got a taste of octopus ink. "For sharks' shake!"

she sputtered, trying to spit the ink out of her mouth.

"Kiki has purple lips," Rocky teased.

Mrs. Karp looked up from her marble desk and glanced around the classroom. "Are you all right, Miss Coral?" she asked. Everyone was hard at work on their poems except for Rocky and Kiki.

"Yes," Kiki said, sputtering out the last of the ink.

All day Kiki worried about Nestor. As the class lined up for lunch, she thought about the bear's cute black nose. As she went through the cafeteria's food line, she remembered the bear's tears. By the time she sat down at her corner table with Echo and Shelly, Kiki was so sad that she felt like crying. She stared at her paddle-worm pizza in silence.

"Guess what?" Pearl floated up to their table. "Tonight is the night I get to see the Rays in Poseidon! My dad said the tickets cost a bundle, but it will be so worth it!"

Kiki knew the jewels Pearl's dad had spent on Rays tickets probably would have paid to get Nestor home on a manta ray. It made Kiki so mad, she snapped at Pearl, "There are more important things in this ocean than seeing a silly concert!"

"Sweet seaweed!" Pearl cried. "What's wrong with *you*?"

"She's upset because we found a lost baby

polar bear and we're trying to find a way to get him home," Echo explained.

"A polar bear in Trident City!" Pearl screeched. "Is that safe?"

"Of course it's safe," Kiki told her. "He's just a lost baby."

Pearl frowned and drifted off to her own table of merfriends.

"Pearl makes me so mad sometimes," Kiki admitted.

"Forget about her," Shelly said. "Let's think about how we can earn some jewels."

Most things in Trident City only cost a few shells, but more expensive things cost at least one jewel. It took a lot of shells to equal one jewel. The Manta Ray Express trip to get Nestor home would cost a whopping four jewels—a fortune!

"What if we had a bake sale?" Echo said. "I bet Crystal would help us make some crab popovers." Crystal was Echo's older sister.

"That's a good idea," Shelly agreed. "And maybe we could have a shell wash, too."

"What did you say?" Kiki asked Shelly.

"A shell wash," Shelly explained. "We could offer to scrub scum off people's homes in exchange for shells."

"A shell wash and a bake sale are great ideas, but we need a lot of jewels fast." Kiki paused and glanced over at Pearl. She was waving her arms around, telling all the other merkids about the Rays concert.

Kiki's face lit up. "And I just thought of how to do it!" she squealed.

She splashed away from the lunch table and over to Pearl. "Thanks!" Kiki said, giving Pearl a great big hug. "Without you I'd have never thought of a way to save the polar bear."

Pearl pushed away from Kiki and frowned. "What are you talking about?"

Shelly and Echo swam up beside Kiki. "What *are* you talking about?" Echo asked.

"Meet me in the front hallway after school," Kiki said. "Pearl gave me a great idea. I know how to get the jewels to send Nestor home!"

8

Last Hope

"ALL WE HAVE TO DO IS convince the Rays to perform a mini concert," Kiki explained to Echo and Shelly. "Everyone will pay for tickets to see them, and we can use those shells and jewels to send Nestor home on the Manta Ray Express. It's called a fund-raiser! My mom had one to raise money for our local merhospital."

It was after school, and the huge front hallway of Trident Academy was filled with merkids. Some leaned against the shell walls and chatted with friends. Others scurried toward the exit or to their dorm rooms. One group of fifth-grade girls played jump rope with an olive sea snake.

"There's only one problem," Shelly said. "How are we going to get the Rays to do that? We don't even know where they are."

"Oh yes, we do," Echo said with a big smile. "At dinner last night, my mom mentioned that the Rays are staying at the Trident City Plaza Hotel. They must be in town for the concert in Poseidon tonight."

"Really?" Kiki asked, her eyes getting wide.

The Plaza was the fanciest hotel in the entire ocean—and it just happened to be in their city. Echo's mom worked at the Conservatory for the Preservation of Sea Horses and Swordfish, which was inside the hotel.

"Oh my Neptune!" Shelly exclaimed. "What are we waiting for? Let's go find them."

The mergirls stopped just long enough to give Nestor a snack, leaving a trail of bubbles behind as they swam through the Plaza's courtyard and entered the grand hotel. Kiki stopped short and gazed at the shining brass walls and polished green marble floors. Everything sparkled! But Echo and Shelly were used to the hotel, since they had visited Echo's mother at work many times before.

"Come on, let's ask Leroy at the desk," Echo said. "He knows everything."

"Hi, Echo!" a big, burly merman with a fat mustache said cheerfully. He floated behind an enormous brass-and-marble check-in desk.

"Hi, Leroy! Can you tell us which room the Rays are staying in?" Echo asked.

Leroy shook his head. "No wavy way. It's top secret."

"But Leroy," Echo said. "We need them to help with our fund-raiser."

"It's a matter of life or death," Kiki added.

"Never mind," Shelly said, pulling her merfriends away from the counter.

"What do you mean, never mind?" Echo asked. "We need—"

"I think I know where they are," Shelly whispered. "Come on! This way."

Shelly led the mergirls behind a Big Rock Café delivery merguy.

"Why are we following him?" Kiki pointed to the delivery merguy.

"Remember at the beginning of the school year when we saw the Rays at the Big Rock Café?" Shelly asked.

Echo grinned as she realized what Shelly was saying. "They were all drinking Big Swishes!"

Sure enough, the delivery merguy they were following carried four Big Swishes. He led them down a hallway to a door that was guarded by two huge mermen.

"Delivery for the Rays," the merguy squeaked.

"We'll take it to them," a guard said after paying for the drinks.

Kiki swam up to the other guard and said, "We'd like to see the Rays, please. It's an urgent matter."

"No one gets to see the Rays!" the guard snapped. "Besides, they are getting ready for their concert in Poseidon."

"But it's about a fund-raiser for a lost polar bear," Shelly explained.

"It doesn't matter. No one gets to see the Rays," the guard repeated, glaring at them.

Echo asked, "Can you tell Alden that his friend Shelly is here?"

Shelly turned bright red when Echo pointed at her. "Shelly actually sang with him. He will want to see her."

"Echo!" Shelly whispered. "What if he doesn't even remember me?"

"He will," Kiki said. At least she hoped he remembered singing with Shelly at Pearl's birthday party.

The guard grumpily agreed to deliver Echo's message. In just a few merminutes, the four cute merstars appeared in the hallway. Kiki's heart pounded. It was hard to believe she was face-to-face with such famous mersingers.

"Hi, Shelly. Good to see you and your friends," Alden said. The other Rays—Teddy, Harmon, and Ellis—smiled beside him.

Kiki was nervous to speak to the adorable merboys! But thinking of Nestor's sad face gave her courage, so she took a deep breath and said, "It's good to see you, too. We have a huge favor to ask you. A baby polar bear is lost, and we're trying to raise money to send him home on the Manta Ray Express."

"We were wondering if you could sing a few songs to help us," Shelly finished.

Teddy looked at Alden. Alden looked at Harmon, and Ellis looked at Teddy. Kiki held her breath.

The Rays were her last hope. If they wouldn't help, she didn't know how she could get Nestor home. Kiki couldn't believe what Alden said next.

9 The Best Idea Ever

THE NEXT MORNING KIKI woke up early and went to see Nestor. But he wasn't swimming in his usual spot near the Manta Ray Express Station. Kiki closed her eyes and tried to make a vision appear like Madame Hippocampus had shown her. Was Nestor still on his ice floating on the surface above? Or had the ice already melted? Nestor had said it had been getting smaller and smaller every day. But right now Kiki couldn't see anything!

"Oh, Nestor," Kiki moaned. *"Are you all right?"*

Just then a white paw with black toenails tapped Kiki's shoulder. It was Nestor!

"Kiki, my ice is almost gone," he whispered. *"What am I going to do?"*

Kiki gulped and looked into the bear's big, dark eyes. *"Don't worry. I have the best news! We made a plan to get you home."*

She hugged Nestor and gave him the parrot-fish pancakes she had saved from breakfast. He swallowed them down in one bite before lunging toward the water's surface. Kiki thought the little bear looked awfully skinny. She was worried he wasn't getting enough to eat, but it was hard to sneak food from the cafeteria without anyone seeing her. They had to get him home fast.

Kiki raced to Trident Academy and almost bumped into Pearl right outside. "Hi, Pearl," Kiki said. "How was the concert last night?"

Pearl frowned at Kiki. "The concert was fantastic, but I couldn't believe my ears when the Rays said they were performing tonight at the People Museum!"

Kiki nodded. "Yes, isn't it wavy? They're helping us with a fund-raiser to send the

baby polar bear home. Shelly's grandfather agreed to let us have a Rays concert in the museum's main hall."

Pearl's face got really red. "But my father paid all that money so that *I* could see the Rays in Poseidon! Now anyone in Trident City can see them for a lot less."

Kiki shrugged. "Sorry."

"Sorry my tail!" Pearl snapped. "After school I'm going to go to the Shark Patrol and tell them all about that dangerous polar bear! They'll have to lock it up! Then just try to have your silly fund-raiser."

"No!" Kiki gasped. "You can't."

"Just you wait and see. They'll put that nasty bear someplace where it can't bother us merfolk. And the Rays will probably thank me for keeping our water safe! Then I can give them my poem song."

"But Nestor is only a baby! He would never hurt anyone. And we have to send him home, not lock him up," Kiki begged.

But Pearl wouldn't listen. She soared past dozens of merstudents to her classroom.

Shelly and Echo touched Kiki on the

back. "We heard what happened," Shelly said. "Why is Pearl being so mean?"

"Because she's Pearl!" Echo said sadly.

"What are we going to do?" Kiki moaned. When the Rays had agreed to help Nestor, Kiki thought that their troubles were over. Now the Shark Patrol might take the polar bear away before they could even have the concert!

"We're not going to give up," Shelly said. "I may not have visions, but I do have a feeling that if we keep working on the concert, everything is going to turn out totally wavy."

Kiki hoped Shelly was right.

Later in class Kiki tried to keep her mind on schoolwork, but she couldn't stop thinking about Pearl's threat. Would she really go to the Shark Patrol? What if they did something horrible to Nestor?

Kiki had stayed up very late the night before making posters about the concert, which she had hung all over school. At lunchtime, every merkid in the cafeteria was whispering about them. Every merkid except Pearl, that is. She just glared at Kiki.

"I'm totally going to be there," Rocky bragged. "Maybe I'll even get to go onstage with the Rays. After all, my dad is the mayor of Trident City."

After lunch, Mrs. Karp made an announcement. "All poems must be finished today. You may use some class time to work on yours."

When Kiki had to sharpen her sea quill pen at the quill sharpener, she floated by Pearl's desk. Pearl was hard at work on her poem song. And that was when Kiki got an idea. It was a fabulous, stupendous idea. In fact, it was the best idea ever!

10 Totally Wavy

"I WONDER WHEN PEARL IS GOING to the Shark Patrol," Echo said to Kiki and Shelly after school. They were floating in Trident Academy's huge front hallway with hundreds of other students.

"Do you want me to talk to her?" Shelly

asked. “Maybe I can keep her busy until after the concert.”

Kiki smiled. She knew her friends would help in any way they could. “Nope. I think I have the Pearl problem taken care of—at least, I hope so.”

“How?” Echo asked in surprise.

“I’ll tell you later. Right now let’s get to the People Museum and help collect money!” Kiki replied.

Echo, Kiki, and Shelly had worked very hard the evening before to transform the museum into a concert hall, adding hundreds of rock seats and even a small stage. Luckily, Grandfather Siren had everything they needed in his many storage closets. And Echo’s dad, who owned Reef’s

Store, had donated stoplight loosejaw fish that would put spotlights on the singers. Echo's mom and Crystal had even volunteered to sell tickets.

"It's so wonderful that everyone is pulling together to help Nestor," Kiki said, wiping a happy tear from her eye as they swam through MerPark. "I just hope we can raise enough shells to send him home."

Even though the concert wasn't going to begin for several hours, Grandfather Siren had told them that merpeople would show up early to get the best seats, and he was right. When they arrived at the museum, a line had already formed outside the door.

Kiki was so surprised! Almost every merkid and teacher from Trident Academy was there. Mrs. Karp was one of the first in line! And Kiki had to blink several times before she could believe her eyes: Pearl was there too! After how mad she had been at school earlier, Kiki didn't think Pearl would come. Before long the entire museum was full; they even had to turn merfolk away.

"Oh no!" Echo said, pointing toward the Manta Ray station. Three serious-looking guards swam toward them. "Pearl sent the Shark Patrol after all."

But the large guards weren't there to lock up Nestor. "We heard about the fund-raiser and we'd like to help. No baby—even a polar bear—should be lost. Do you need us to control the crowd?" one of them asked.

"Sure," Kiki said. She was so happy that the guards weren't going to take Nestor away that she felt like giving them a great big hug.

There was only one problem: the Rays hadn't arrived yet. Had they forgotten? Had they changed their minds?

Suddenly Kiki's eyes grew cloudy and her ears felt like they were clogged. She was having another vision! In her mind she saw the Rays above her, with something large and white floating between them. After the vision passed and her mind was blank again, she looked up.

"There they are!"

The Rays were swimming down from the water's surface. With them was Nestor!

"We thought that the polar bear should be the star of this show," Alden said.

"At least for a few minutes," Teddy added as he winked at Kiki. Kiki's heart skipped a beat. He was *so* cute and *so* sweet!

When the Rays and Nestor went inside the museum, the whole crowd cheered. Shelly, Echo, and Kiki stood to the side of the makeshift stage, while mergirls screamed and threw sea tulips at the four merstars. Kiki was glad the guards were there to help tame the rowdy audience.

"Let's hear it for Nestor!" Alden yelled. "He's the reason we're here!"

A huge roar of approval came from the crowd. A girl's voice rang out, "We love polar bears!" Kiki giggled when she saw that it was her classmate Wanda who'd yelled.

Nestor waved as he floated back toward the surface. The Rays sang "Shake Your Tail," along with "Shark, the Sharpnose Sevengill" and their first big hit, "Oh, Barracuda."

When the Rays finished performing, everyone clapped and cheered. Pearl's voice squealed above the rest, "I love you, Teddy!" The guards helped the Rays get away from the crowd.

Kiki, Echo, and Shelly met the cute merboy band backstage. It was time to count the number of shells they had raised. Would they have enough to buy a ticket to the Arctic Ocean?

Kiki's tail was trembling as she and her merfriends counted the shells. What if they didn't have enough? What would they do then?

But they *did* it! They had collected enough shells to equal four jewels—the exact amount needed to send Nestor home.

"This is fin-tastic!" Kiki squealed.

"Come on," Harmon said, grabbing Kiki's hand. "We have a polar bear to save!"

The seven of them swam over to the Manta Ray Express Station. Kiki bought a first-class private ticket for Nestor on the largest ray available.

"Don't worry," the agent said. "We'll get your little polar bear home faster than a humpback can breach."

Echo giggled. "It'll be a polar bear express!"

Nestor dived down from the surface and climbed aboard the ray. The bear waved and waved. *"Thanks, my merbuddies!"* he called as the ray zoomed toward the surface and the bear's home.

"Bye, my polar buddy," Kiki said, with a tear in her eye. As happy as she was that Nestor was going home, she was going to miss her furry friend.

When Nestor was gone, Shelly tapped Kiki on the shoulder. "Now will you tell us how you changed Pearl's mind about sending the Shark Patrol after Nestor?"

"Oh!" Kiki gasped. "Thanks for reminding me. I almost forgot!" She pulled a folded piece of seaweed from her orange shell purse and handed it to Alden.

"What's this?" he asked.

"It's a poem song written for you by one of our classmates, Pearl Swamp," Kiki explained. "I promised her I'd give it to you." She turned to her friends. "And in return," she whispered, "Pearl promised to leave Nestor alone."

Alden glanced down at the words and started humming a tune. "Hey, this isn't bad."

Kiki grinned. "If you like it, maybe you can make it your next song."

Echo rolled her eyes. "If you do, Pearl will be bragging for the rest of her life."

Kiki laughed. She didn't care if Pearl

did brag. She was just glad that Nestor was on his way home. She closed her eyes. In her mind, she had a vision of the little bear and his mother hugging. It was her favorite vision of all.

"Are you all right?" Shelly asked Kiki.

"Yes, I am totally wavy!" Kiki told her. And she was.

POLAR PAL (AN ACROSTIC POEM)

By Shelly Siren

Playful friend

Our polar buddy

Lost and hungry

Away we go to

Rescue our pal

PEOPLE DREAMS (A CINQUAIN POEM)

By Echo Reef

Humans

Mysterious

I dream of seeing one

Do you think a human wants to

See me?

FOOD FIGHTS (A HAIKU POEM)

By Rocky Ridge

Food fights can be fun

Especially at lunchtime

Splat! Right in the face!

LOVE PIRATE
(FREE VERSE FOR A RAYS SONG)

By Pearl Swamp

Hidden deep beneath the sea

A secret lies with me

Treasures rich beyond compare

But do I dare?

Love pirate

You are a love pirate

Will you steal my heart?

Or bring me gold?

LOST (A HAIKU POEM)

By Kiki Coral

My polar buddy

So lost in the great ocean

He needs a way home.

The Mermaid Tales Song

REFRAIN:

Let the water roar

Deep down we're swimming along

Twirling, swirling, singing the mermaid song.

VERSE 1:

Shelly flips her tail

Racing, diving, chasing a whale

Twirling, swirling, singing the mermaid song.

VERSE 2:

Pearl likes to shine

Oh my Neptune, she looks so fine

Twirling, swirling, singing the mermaid song.

VERSE 3:

Shining Echo flips her tail

Backward and forward without fail

Twirling, swirling, singing the mermaid song.

VERSE 4:

Amazing Kiki

Far from home and floating so free

Twirling, swirling, singing the mermaid song

Author's Note

WHEN I WAS YOUNG, I passed by the same poster every Sunday. I read the poem on the poster each time I walked by. It was:

I never saw a moor,
I never saw the sea;
Yet know I how the heather looks,
And what a wave must be.

I never spoke with God,

Nor visited in heaven;

Yet certain am I of the spot

As if the chart were given.

Because I read it every week, I learned this Emily Dickinson poem by heart. Maybe you can do the same thing. Write a poem out and hang it on your wall. Read it every day and soon you'll remember it by heart, even when you are old like me!

Hope you'll have a good time trying to write your own poems too. Visit my website, www.debbiedadey.com, for more writing fun.

Your mermaid friend,

Debbie Dadey

Glossary

BARRACUDA: The fast great barracuda has needle-sharp teeth and a long body. Eating even a tiny bite of barracuda meat can make a human sick.

CRAB: The tiny pea crab lives inside a mussel shell and eats the plankton that gets trapped inside.

DOLPHIN: Bottlenose dolphins are often seen following ships and even bodysurfing on the ships' waves.

LONGHORN COWFISH: This fish gets its

name from the long, fleshy horns above its eyes.

MANTA RAY: The manta ray is the largest of all the rays. It can grow up to twenty-six feet from the tip of one wing to the other. Luckily, it only eats plankton and small fish.

OCTOPUS: The Dumbo octopus lives in the deep sea and has two large fins that look like ears.

OLIVE SEA SNAKE: This snake lives in the water near Australia. It has short fangs and toxic venom.

PADDLE WORM: This green worm lives in shallow water and on the shore. If you see something green about the size of a marble near the water, it might be a cluster of paddle-worm eggs.

PARROT FISH: This brightly colored fish has teeth that form a parrotlike beak.

POLAR BEAR: The polar bear is the largest bear. Polar bears are good swimmers and have an excellent sense of smell.

PUFFER FISH: If something scares a puffer fish, it will swallow water and blow up to a much larger size.

RIBBON WORMS: This worm can grow as long as a football field is wide!

SEA CUCUMBERS: Deep-sea cucumbers are like vacuum cleaners on the bottom of the ocean. They are colorless but glow all over with bioluminescent light.

SEA HORSES: The male sea horse has a pouch, somewhat like that of a kangaroo. The sea horse carries eggs in the pouch until they hatch.

SEA SLUG: The Hermissenda sea slug should be called the porcupine sea slug. It saves the stinging cells from any creature it captures. The Hermissenda puts the stinging cells on its own back for protection.

SEA SQUIRT: The colonial sea squirt lives in urn-shaped colonies and has a green color.

SEA TULIP: The sea tulip is a type of giant sea squirt that has a long stalk. Its body is on the end of the stalk and is bright yellow.

SEA TURTLE: The loggerhead turtle is the second-largest marine turtle. It eats crabs, lobsters, and clams.

SEAWEED: Seaweed does not have roots, but floats freely.

SHARPNOSE SEVENGILL SHARK: This deepwater shark has a pointed snout and is an endangered species.

SHORE CLINGFISH: This small fish can cling to rocks with a powerful sucker formed from its fins. Its snout looks like a duck's bill.

STARFISH: Most starfish have five arms. If one of their arms is lost, they can regrow it!

STOPLIGHT LOOSEJAW: This deep-sea fish's mouth doesn't have a bottom. This fish has large photophores under each eye to create a light show.

SWORDFISH: The upper jawbone of a swordfish looks a lot like a sword.

WHALE: The blue whale is the largest animal that has ever lived. It can eat more than 6,600 pounds of food a day!

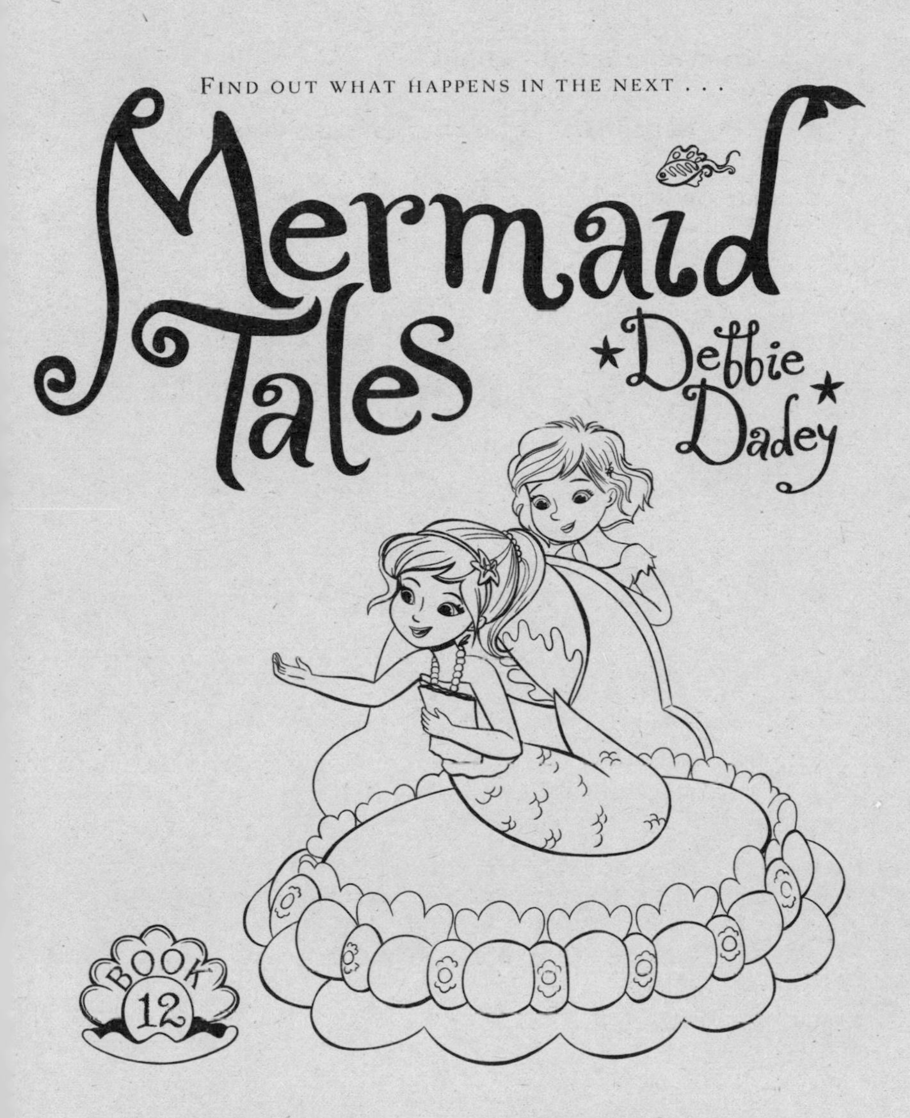

Wish upon a Starfish

1

The Sound of Waves

"BRAVO!"

The crowd cheered and clapped as Pearl Swamp took a bow. Her diamond-studded costume billowed around her gold tail on the sparkling stage. Members of the audience whistled and tossed her beautiful bouquets of sea lavender.

Pearl waved as merfolk from all over the ocean cried out, "We love you, Pearl!" and "You are the best actress in the whole merworld!"

She couldn't believe her good luck. A famous director had picked her out of all the merstudents at Trident Academy to star as Fishlein Maria in his play *The Sound of Waves*. As the curtain closed, a crowd of fans and reporters rushed to Pearl's side.

"Miss Swamp, may I have my picture sketched with you?" asked a small mergirl.

Pearl nodded and lifted her pointy nose in the water as the merartist Piddock Picasso sketched her on a piece of kelp for her fan.

"May I have an interview?" asked *Trident City Tide* reporter Lulu Lampern.

"Of course," Pearl said, waving away the hundreds of merpeople still waiting to have their picture drawn with her. Others floated nearby, holding sea pens and seaweed, hoping Pearl would sign autographs.

"How does it feel to be famous?" Lulu asked.

Pearl smiled. "It is fabulous and everything I dreamed it would be."

Lulu scribbled some notes on seaweed before looking up. "What is your favorite part of being a star?"

"There is nothing more fin-tastic than knowing an audience is cheering for me,"

Pearl said. "It is an amazing feeling!" She paused before adding, "Of course, the jewels and flowers are nice too."

"You were simply mervelous in the play tonight," Lulu said. "And we look forward to seeing you in many more. I'll let you get back to your fans now. Thanks."

Pearl nodded and turned toward a huge crowd. They were all chanting, "Pearl! Pearl!"

One screaming fan even broke through the crowd and tried to hug Pearl. Then the fan began shaking Pearl's shoulders.

"What are you doing?" Pearl cried. "Stop that right now!"

"Pearl! Pearl! Wake up, my little pupfish!"

Pearl's eyes popped open. She wasn't surrounded by screaming fans. Instead she was in her bed, surrounded by a curtain of daisy coral, and the person shaking her shoulders was her mother!

"Pearl, you must have been having a dream. It's time for school."

Pearl hugged her mother. "I dreamed I was a famous meractress," she explained. "A real star of the sea!"

"You are always a sea star to me!" Mrs. Swamp said, kissing the top of Pearl's head. "Now, come to breakfast. The mercook made water-flea waffles this morning."

Pearl jumped up and ran a Venus comb through her hair. Her dream had felt so real: the screaming fans, the flowers, and the beautiful costumes on the glittering stage. Pearl's greatest wish was to become a star someday—and that day couldn't come soon enough!

2 Angelfish Molie

PEARL YAWNED AS SHE POURED sandweed syrup on her water-flea waffles. She took a big bite and looked at her father. Mr. Swamp was reading the newsweed while sipping his favorite copepod coffee. Usually Pearl didn't read the *Trident City Tide* because she found most of its news stories quite dull. But this time she squealed when she saw the back of her father's kelp.

"Oh my Neptune!" Pearl shouted. "Angelfish Molie is coming to Trident City!"

Mr. Swamp was so startled by Pearl's shout that he spilled coffee all over his gold-and-black-striped tail. "What are you yelling about so early in the morning?" he asked, using his kelp napkin to wipe up the mess.

"You're always telling me I should keep up with the local news, so I read the back of the *Trident City Tide.*" Pearl pointed to an article that said that Angelfish Molie, the most famous meractress in all the ocean, would be starring in *Gone with the Tide* at the Grand Banks Theater. And the play was opening Tuesday night—tomorrow evening!

"Please, Daddy," Pearl begged. "Can you take me to see her?" Dreaming about being famous was fun, but actually seeing a star perform in person would be totally wavy.

Mr. Swamp nodded. "I'll see if I can get tickets."

Pearl threw herself at her father and gave him a big hug, overturning her water-flea waffles in the process.

"I can't wait to tell Wanda!" Pearl shrieked. "This is the most exciting thing that has ever happened in the history of Trident City!"

Pearl dressed for school in record time and soared through the water to Trident Academy. She found her best friend, Wanda Slug, waiting for her in the school's huge front entrance hall.

"Pearl!" Wanda called. "I have wonderful news!"

"Is it about Angelfish Molie?" Pearl asked.

Wanda shook her head. "No, this is much better."

Pearl could not imagine anything being more wonderful than getting to see the most famous meractress in the ocean.

"What's better than Angelfish Molie?" Pearl demanded.

"This!" Wanda exclaimed, pointing to a sign hanging nearby.

Pearl cheered when she read the announcement.

TRIDENT ACADEMY'S THIRD-GRADE
CLASS PROUDLY PRESENTS

The Little Human

A PLAY IN TWO ACTS

TRYOUTS WEDNESDAY
IN FINN AUDITORIUM!
QUESTIONS? SEE MRS. J. KARP

Debbie Dadey

is the author and coauthor of more than one hundred and fifty children's books, including the series The Adventures of the Bailey School Kids. A former teacher and librarian, Debbie and her family split their time between Bucks County, Pennsylvania, and Sevierville, Tennessee. She hopes you'll visit www.debbiedadey.com for lots of mermaid fun.

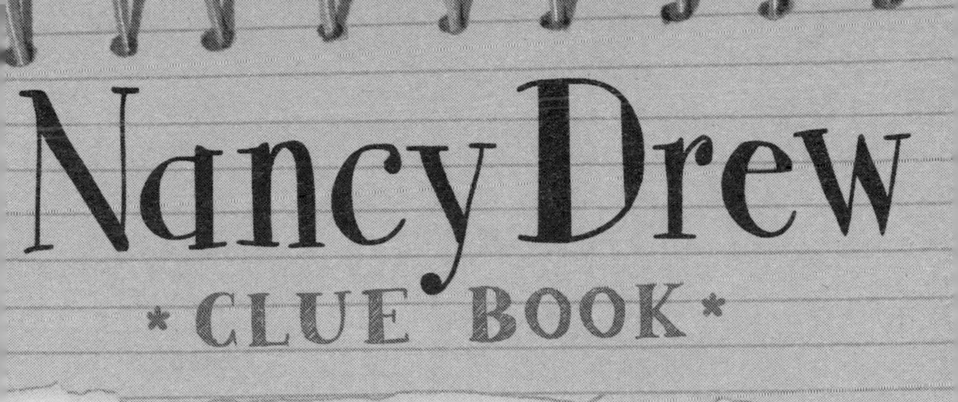

Test your detective skills with Nancy and her best friends, Bess and George!

NancyDrew.com

 Chocolate Dreams	 Rainbow Swirl	 Caramel Moon	 Cool Mint	 Magic Hearts	 Gooey Goblins
The Sugar Ball	A Valentine's Surprise	 Bubble Gum Rescue	 Double Dip	 Jelly Bean Jumble	The Chocolate Rose
 A Royal Wedding	 Marshmallow Mystery	 Frozen Treats	 The Sugar Cup	 Sweet Secrets	 Taffy Trouble

Visit candyfairies.com for games, recipes, and more!

EBOOK EDITIONS ALSO AVAILABLE

FROM ALADDIN • KIDS.SIMONANDSCHUSTER.COM